The Quilt

Books by T. Davis Bunn

The Quilt
The Gift
The Messenger

The Maestro
The Presence
Promises to Keep
Riders of the Pale Horse

The Priceless Collection
Secret Treasures of Eastern Europe

1. *Florian's Gate*
2. *The Amber Room*
3. *Winter Palace*

Rendezvous With Destiny

1. *Rhineland Inheritance*
2. *Gibraltar Passage*
3. *Sahara Crosswind*
4. *Berlin Encounter*
5. *Istanbul Express*

The Quilt

T. Davis Bunn

BETHANY HOUSE PUBLISHERS
MINNEAPOLIS, MINNESOTA 55438

Originally published under the same title in England in 1992 by Monarch Publications.

Copyright © 1993
T. Davis Bunn
All Rights Reserved

Published by Bethany House Publishers
A Ministry of Bethany Fellowship, Inc.
11300 Hampshire Avenue South
Minneapolis, Minnesota 55438

Printed in the United States of America

Library of Congress Cataloging-in-Publication Data

Bunn, T. Davis, 1952
    The quilt / T. Davis Bunn.
       p.   cm.

    1. Grandmothers—Fiction.   2. Quilting—Fiction
I. Title.
PS3552.U4718Q55   1993
813'.54—dc20   93–2413
ISBN 1–55661–345–8   CIP

*This book is dedicated
to the memory of my
grandmothers*

*Alice Coats Smith
Maude Davis Bunn*

and to my mother

Becky Bunn

with love and thanksgiving.

Light is sown for the righteous,
And gladness for the upright in heart.
Rejoice in the Lord, ye righteous;
And give thanks at the remembrance
of his holiness.

PSALMS 97:11–12 KJV

NCE UPON A TIME, not so very long ago, there was a little girl who grew up and had a family and tried to raise it as she thought the Lord would want. After a while, in the ways of this earth, she found herself growing old. The seasons seemed to whirl by with ever-increasing speed. The older she became, the harder it was to stop and savor each little moment, because all the moments that had come before were now ganging up on her, pushing her with ever greater pressure toward that final door. Life's current became so swift that the days and weeks and months which used to mark her passage no longer held any meaning. They all flowed together

into a kindly pastel blur, with little flecks of light every now and then to illuminate the world before her failing eyes. Grandchildren were born, other little girls to help take the first fragile steps upon life's way. Lifetime friends passed on to that higher ground, their absence like vacuums in her world. And the faster the currents seemed to flow, the more still she seemed to become. All her remaining energy became focused on that which lay ahead.

There came a time when her hands grew swollen and twisted by arthritis. She would look down at them and have difficulty seeing them as they were. Somewhere deep inside, she knew, was captured the fragile beauty of a seventeen-year-old farm girl who had given her life in holy matrimony to a man now eleven years in the grave. Sometimes she would look away from the window by which she sat, or look down from the television that

kept her company between visits of her beloved family, and she would knead and squeeze her hands, one with the other.

There were so many skills within those hands, so many memories, so many stories to tell. And something would touch her heart then, a gentle yearning, the whisper of a melody she would strain and still not be able to hear. It was like waking in the middle of the night, lying there in her lonely darkness, staring at the ceiling overhead, and listening to the laughter of children who had now

grown up to have children of their own. Yet she could still hear her young children and feel them so close that it was almost as though they were there in the room with her. Exactly what it was they said, she could not make out. But somehow she felt it was important, as though these gentle ghosts of a time long gone were there to remind her of something. And during her days, as she sat and pressed and kneaded her fingers, she would hear a gentle voice calling to her. There was something left undone.

When the neighbors talked of her, which was often, they all used one word to describe her. The word was *beautiful*.

They would even say it to her face, some of them. "Mary, you are the most beautiful woman I've ever laid eyes on." And they'd mean it.

Her reply was always the same. "Honey, your eyes are worse than mine." Then she'd

peel off her trifocals, blink in that fragile way
of very old ladies and pass her glasses over,
saying, "Here, see if they help you any."

And the people would always laugh and
change the subject, wishing there was some
better way to tell her what the feeling was
they had right then in their hearts.

Even Everett, her son the businessman,
would come in and sit longer and quieter
than he'd ever sat in his life. Wednesday
morning was Everett's time, on account of his
having to be at the farm-machinery auction
on that side of town. He'd come in and pour
himself a cup of coffee and lean over and kiss
his mother very self-consciously on the forehead. Everett had always been self-conscious
about any show of emotion. His wife had
once confided to Mary that Everett was the
only man she'd ever met who could get red
in the face hearing the preacher talk about
love.

"Everett is about the strangest child I've ever seen," Mary replied.

"You mean *was* the strangest child," Lou Ann, Everett's wife, corrected.

"I mean just exactly what I said. That man has still got a three-year-old child walking around inside him. Don't know a single man that doesn't." Mary lowered her head so as to get Everett's wife fixed inside the proper lens of her trifocals. "That's the only thing that makes most men worth living with, fact that they've got a little bit of the little boy inside them. Keep that little boy laughing and you've got a happy man on your hands."

Lou Ann took that and told it all over town. And everybody she talked to shook their heads and smiled and said something like, yes sir, that's just like Mary, isn't it? That's one of the finest women God ever set on this earth.

Then somebody else would nod like they

12

were thinking it for the very first time and say, yes sir, a real beautiful woman. And no one would dispute it. Of course, they weren't talking about any beauty that you could see. Sometimes somebody would talk about how she'd been a real beauty when she was younger, but it was all hearsay. There was nobody alive anymore who had known Mary as a young girl, except some people as old and doddery as Mary, and they had more sense in their heads than to talk about something that didn't mean two shakes to anybody anymore.

Whatever it was, that beauty kept people stopping by. Friends of her children and their wives and sometimes even their children would stop and say something like, I was over in the neighborhood and I thought maybe I'd just drop in and say hello. It was all just pure silliness, what they said, because Mary didn't live in the neighborhood of anybody except a couple of tobacco farms and the town's dairy. But like most people, they were embarrassed to say what was on their minds—or even admit it to themselves.

And these visiting women would prop up their children on their laps and hope that the young ones would behave, because for some reason that they couldn't explain, what Mary thought about their children was very important. And Mary would smile a little smile that barely turned up the edges of her mouth but brought such warmth to her eyes that even the most rambunctious of children would quiet down and smile back. And she would reach out one shaky bent hand and run a finger down the side of the young one's face and then say something like, I believe there's some homemade butterscotch in that jar in the kitchen by the window. Can you be a big boy and lift off that top real careful? And the child might not even know what

homemade butterscotch tasted like, but there was something about Mary that made them pretty doggone sure that whatever it was, it was good. So they'd make round moon-eyes and nod solemnly, and if they were real polite they might even answer with the best yes, ma'am. Then Mary would run her finger down their cheek one more time, as though she was trying to draw a little of their beauty and joy out and hold it in her own hand. Go on then, she'd say. And when you go back outside, mind you stay off the grape arbor.

The mothers would have some question they'd probably thought up on the way out there, like, I just had to have your recipe for homemade peach jam. Or maybe it was, I can't seem to get my lemon chess pies to set up right. Or their husbands would stop by because they thought maybe Mary could use a couple of their extra geraniums, and the wives would just come along for the ride. But sooner or later, the real reason for their visit would come out.

Maybe it was a sick child. Maybe a husband couldn't seem to hold down a steady job. Or perhaps it was some real deep marital problems. There was trouble with loved ones and ones that weren't loved at all, with jobs and houses and money and people. There were worries and fears and doubts and terrors that woke them up in the middle of the night, leaving them teary-eyed and heartsore and sweaty-palmed and shaky. Sooner or later, those problems all came out.

And Mary listened. She didn't often say much, and when she did speak, it wasn't for very long. Mostly she just sat and looked at the person there beside her with those expressive eyes of hers. Even as they swam behind her trifocals, Mary's eyes held more love than most people ever thought existed on this earth. And when it came time to reach out and comfort those burdened with the world's woes, Mary's eyes filled the room with light.

After the words and sometimes the tears had passed, folks tended to sit for a time, sharing in Mary's silence. And when the outside world called them back again, to stoves and jobs and restless children, they carried a bit of Mary's stillness along with them.

The strange thing was, people rarely talked about sitting there with Mary. To their closest friends, they might say something like, I stopped by to see Mary today. She gave me her special recipe for German chocolate layer cake. And they'd smile in an almost embarrassed fashion, as though there was something to be ashamed about in being so touched by something they couldn't put into words. The closest they ever came to explaining it was by describing something external.

For instance, Everett kept telling his wife

17

Lou Ann that he ought to have those seven Bibles his mother kept stacked by her television rebound. They were so ragged and worn with age and use they had to be held together with binder twine. Someday they're gonna be all that is left of that woman, Everett would say, and right then and there Lou Ann would make him stop. She just couldn't bear to imagine a world without Mary.

One young man was just out of seminary school and real worried about getting sent to a good church. He found himself driving out by Mary's one day, kind of meandering all over the county before deciding what he wanted to do with his afternoon. That evening he told a couple of his buddies it had seemed as if the old needlepoint that hung above the hall door, the one that said "In Everything Give Thanks," had shone in his eyes the whole time he'd sat in Mary's front parlor. The next day the young man was real embarrassed about what he'd said, even though nobody'd laughed at him. He promised himself never to talk about stuff like that ever again. He called it conduct unbecoming to a minister.

The first Wednesday after the young minister's visit, Everett stopped by Mary's as usual, to find his elder brother Jonas working out by the woodshed. Jonas was the son who most resembled their father, big and gangly and silent, a real lover of the land. Jonas had stayed where he had been born, building his own farmhouse down at the base of the hill, tilling his garden on land that his father's father had first cleared and planted, making his living as a joiner and cabinetmaker.

Everett stood and watched Jonas for a spell, wondering what brought him up here in the middle of the week, feeling pretty put out that his Wednesday morning routine was being disturbed. Finally he said it, "Jonas, what in Sam Hill are you doing?"

"Momma wants to make a quilt," Jonas said in his quiet, slow-talking way, not even looking up from his work. He handled the wood-planer and hand-sander and hammer as if they were all extensions of his rough-hewn hands.

Everett sucked in the belly that he told everybody had come with his job, on account of his brother standing there all sunburned and rock-solid. He opened his mouth, but closed it again. He didn't know exactly how he could say what was really bothering him, which was that he looked forward all week to having these few moments alone with Mary. He didn't often talk about anything more than what farm prices were doing or some problem he was having in the office. But way down deep inside himself, Everett knew he always walked away from those mornings a better man.

Jonas straightened and wiped a sweaty brow and spoke as though he were reading his brother's mind, "Momma called down this morning, said she wanted me up just soon as I finished my coffee. Told Jody if I wasn't up here in record time she was gonna cut herself a switch."

Everett didn't smile. "That old woman's got no more business starting a quilt than I do flying off to the moon."

21

"You said it," Jonas agreed, and bent back to his work.

Everett watched him and saw the same solid quality taking shape that marked everything Jonas did. Everett stifled a familiar twinge of jealousy as he stood and watched his brother. Everett was the one who had the big house in the city, the fancy car, the office with the swivel-back leather chair, and the two secretaries. His brother worked from dawn to dusk and barely made ends meet. Yet when Jonas turned his hand to something, it was with an artist's skill.

For someone who knew how to make it right, as Jonas did, a quilting frame looked like a child's idea of a four-poster bed without the mattress. The four corner posts stuck up in both directions about the same distance, so that the quilt could either be turned right-side up or upside down or on either end. A quilt required maybe six months of handiwork, so it was important for the quilter to reach every little corner in the most comfortable fashion possible.

There were solid little wooden blocks with big washers and wing nuts all the way around the sides so that the quilt could be stretched out tight, then with a quick flip of the wrist be released. Once the cotton batting was laid out and basted into place, the best place to work on the finer stitching was by the biggest window in the house, sitting in the favorite rocker, with crowds of memories and good thoughts for company. That was the joy of quilting, watching the little raggedy patches of material be joined into a work of timeless beauty and knowing that no matter how many hours were put in today, there were still a hundred days left to do.

"Momma's waiting for you," Jonas finally said. "Better go in 'fore she throws the coffee out."

"I still say she ain't got any business starting a quilt," Everett said and turned on his
heel.

He was barely in the door before he said
to Mary, "You mind telling me what's gotten
into you?"

"You know, I believe there's a mocking-
bird that's decided to nest on my bedroom
windowsill," Mary said, not looking up from
the well-worn book opened in her lap. "Can
you imagine anything nicer than a summer
filled with mockingbirds greeting the
dawn?"

Everett walked into the kitchen and made
as much clatter as he could while pouring a
cup of coffee, just to show Mary how indig-
nant he really was. When he came back into
the sitting room he said, "Momma, I want to
know what you think you're up to here."

With a sigh Mary shut the Bible, careful
to lift it from the back with both hands. "I

thought this one was going to be the one to
see me to the grave, but I declare the pages
fall out if I look at them hard. You think
maybe you could pick me up another Bible?
Maybe one of those with the big letters would
be nice."

"You're not answering my question,
Momma."

"Put down your coffee cup and come over here and kiss me hello."

"Not till you answer me."

Mary tilted her head upward and focused on her son through the trifocals. In her mildest voice she told him, "You're not too old to get a taste of my mind, young man."

Everett didn't waste any more time. Anybody who knew Mary knew that her last warning was always given in her quietest manner. After that it was time to go looking for cover.

"That's better," Mary said once her cheek had been bussed. "Now sit down over there where I can see you and tell me about the family."

Everett sat down with an exaggerated sigh and decided to risk it. "Momma, what on earth do you think you're gonna do? You can't even—"

"Don't you go telling me what I can and

can't do," Mary replied. "There's been something bothering me for almost a year now, something I've left undone. Been searching for it the best part of every night, wondering if maybe the Lord was trying to tell me something."

"But a quilt, Momma," Everett protested. He gave a swift glance at her hands. The arthritis had turned the fingers sideways, so that they stuck out from her palm at this weird angle. Everett didn't like to look at Mary's hands. It always gave him this little twist of pain down in his gut.

"If that's what the Lord wants me to do, son, then that's what I'm gonna do." There was a firmness to Mary's voice that brooked no further argument. "Now tell me about the family."

Everett held his peace in front of Mary, but that evening he really let his wife Lou Ann know what he thought of it all.

"Can you imagine?" Everett pushed his dessert plate back far enough to lean both elbows heavily on the table. "The woman can barely read a big-letter Bible, she's gotta have the television almost in her lap to see it. Fingers all bent over, shoot, I wonder how she'll even be able to pick up a needle. And she thinks she's gonna sew herself another quilt."

Lou Ann thought of the four quilts Mary had already done for them, the big one for their own bed and the three with patches of animal-covered fabrics for the children. "Mary makes the prettiest quilts I ever saw."

"Made, honey. Mary made the prettiest quilts. I didn't say anything about that, now, did I. Not a peep. Wouldn't trade anything for those pretty ones upstairs. Sell my car before I sold my quilt. Wasn't talking about that for a minute. I just don't want the old lady to get disappointed."

Lou Ann knew better than to hit her husband head on with any disagreement when he was in one of his moods. "She tell you how the Lord told her to do the quilt?"

"No, she didn't, and I'll bet you it was because she was afraid I'd show her just how wrong she was to even think it." He picked up the last bit of pie his littlest girl had left on her plate and pushed it in his mouth, then licked his fingers carefully. Lou Ann made just about the best brown sugar pie he'd ever tasted. She'd even managed to improve on the recipe Mary'd given her.

"I don't know, honey." Lou Ann stood and started gathering plates. "Mary's not the type of lady to say it was a message from the Lord when it wasn't."

"Momma's the best woman I know," he said to her retreating back, then added hastily, "except for you, honey. But I do declare she's getting on. You know, she's reached that

point where maybe she's not thinking so clearly anymore."

Lou Ann appeared in the kitchen door-way. "Don't you let her hear you say that."

"What, you think you're married to a crazy man?" Everett asked, rolling his eyes.

Being an intelligent woman who loved her husband very much, Lou Ann hid her smile in the kitchen and held her tongue.

"You know what I love the most about Mary?" Lou Ann told Jody, Jonas's wife, the next morning. "She's always so involved."

"That just about says it all," Jody agreed. "She's just about the most involved woman I've ever met."

But Lou Ann wasn't finished. "You don't ever get the feeling that she's just sitting there on the sidelines watching you go through whatever it is that's ailing you. Mary's right in there with you. When I talk to her, some-times it's like I'm talking right to her heart.

Like there's not a thing between me and all that love."

"Just scoop out all you need and carry it away," Jody added.

"If I was sick, I'd rather go talk with Mary for five minutes than have fifteen doctors work on me all day," Lou Ann's next-door neighbor and best friend, Lynn Forrest, told them. Lou Ann and Mary were the only persons in the whole wide world who still called her Lynn. When her husband, Tommy, had started courting her, he had renamed her Rooster, on account of her red hair, her jerky way of moving, and the fact that her maiden name had been Rosters. Lynn said knowing that she was going to have to hear that for the rest of her life had just about done the marriage in before it had started.

There were five of them gathered in Jody's kitchen that morning. Amy Harris was a friend from down the road, a heavyset woman with the biggest laugh anybody'd ever heard. Her laugh wasn't loud. It was just plain big. When Amy laughed, there was just too much happiness and humor there for anybody within hearing range not to smile. Her friends had the habit of looking over at one another when they heard that big bell-shaped laugh ring out. It gave them something to grin about without being so self-conscious. They would look at one another and chuckle like, there she goes again, Amy's laughing. Can you believe it? Amy didn't mind their laughing at her. It was enough just to have them laugh.

The other woman was a tiny wisp of a lady Lynn's husband Tommy had renamed Tidbit. Her real name was Nancy Starling, and she made up for her lack of size with an energy that was just plain awesome. She stood a full four feet ten inches tall in her lace-up shoes and weighed about as much as a wet breeze. She was a nurse at the hospital where Lynn worked as a physical therapist, and had the tendency to make her patients want to stand at attention in bed when she walked into the room. Nancy needed to stand on her tiptoes to take their temperature when the beds were cranked upright, but even the doctors had long since learned not to cross Nurse Tidbit, as everyone called her behind her back. Tommy's names had a habit of sticking like burrs in a horse's mane.

"That woman is a saint," Nancy said quietly, washing blackberries with a speed that made her hands blur. "Every time I see her I tell myself I wish there was something more I could do for her."

They had been out picking blackberries and were getting ready to make cobbler. They were all itching from redbug bites and stained from forehead to knees with blackberry juice, and all were having an enormously good time. Jody was known for making the best blackberry cobbler in three counties. But the pies were really just an excuse for five good friends to get together and ramble through the woods and laugh and spend a morning catching up on one another's lives.

"It's hard to do anything for Mary," Jody agreed, pressing out a dozen mounds of piecrust batter with her rolling pin. One of the secrets of her cobbler was that the crust was made with butter-cookie dough. "She makes me feel like a little girl playing with her mother's things whenever I say I'd like to help her with something."

"Maybe so," Lou Ann said. "But just the same I'm worried about her this time. She's too old to be taking on a quilt by herself."

"Maybe if we all went together she'd listen to us," Nancy said doubtfully.

"We'll take up one of the cobblers and talk

to her," Jody decided for all of them.

But it sure as goodness wasn't all easy street, taking a fresh-baked pie or cake into Mary's house. She was the legendary baker to three generations. The highest accolade a cake or pie could receive was, you've been taking lessons up at Mary's, haven't you?

Mary rarely said anything when somebody brought baked goods by. She'd just sit and smile her heartfelt smile, take a little silver pie fork, and taste the first tiny sliver. The guest would slide up close to the edge of her chair and hold her breath. Mary would take this teensy bite, close her eyes a minute, open them, and smile again. That gave the guest signal to smile back—which was pretty hard, what with their heart in their throat and their palms slick. Then came the verdict. If Mary put the cake down, it was back to the kitchen, girl, and try again. But if she took another bite, well, rest assured there was a winner here.

So Jody was understandably worried when she walked up the long-hill drive from her home to Mary's. Unconsciously the others all kind of pulled in behind her. But their worries were forgotten when they walked into Mary's sitting room and found her sorting through a pile of beautiful old clothes.

"Been up since dawn washing all these old things," Mary said in greeting. "That after spending half the night trying to remember where I stored them."

In Mary's typically neat fashion, the quilt frame was set up against the far wall, as much out of the way as a seven-by-seven wood frame with three-foot corner-posts could be in a formal sitting parlor. Especially a frame which was fitted with a stretch of the prettiest pastel-blue cotton backing any of the ladies had ever seen.

"I brought you a home-made blackberry cobbler," Jody said, her eyes caught by the frame and the backing. "Momma, where on earth did you get that beautiful cloth?"

"Bless your heart, child, just put it on the kitchen cabinet and we'll have it in a bit." Mary straightened from the pile with a grimace and a hand pressing hard on her back. "Been bent over for too long, I reckon."

"You ought to sit down for a while," Jody said, handing the pie to Nancy and hurrying over.

To their surprise Mary did not object. She let herself be led over and seated by the window. All she said was, "Got an awful lot of work ahead of me."

Jody knelt beside the chair. "Momma, you just have to let us help you with this."

"Isn't that pretty cloth?" Mary said in reply, looking over at the quilt frame. "It came to me late last night. I found that, oh, it must be five years ago if it's a day. You remember

old Mrs. Lane, used to run that fabric shop downtown?"

" 'Course I do, Momma, but it was more than five years. Mrs. Lane passed away, my goodness, it must be ten or eleven years now."

"Whenever. It was just before she closed that pretty shop of hers. She came by for coffee one day and gave me that fabric you see over there. Said she'd been saving it for someone special."

Amy walked over to the quilt frame, ran her hand down the cloth and exclaimed, "Will you just come over here and feel this? That's the softest cotton I've ever seen."

"Feels like velvet," Nancy agreed.

"What is it, Miss Mary, some mixture with silk thread?"

"I'm sure I don't know. All I remember is what Mrs. Lane said to me. The first time she felt it, she knew it'd make somebody a very special quilt. Mrs. Lane planned to use it her-

self, but what with one thing and another she never got around to it." Mary was quiet for a very long time. "It just came to me. Wasn't more than a week after she gave me this material that we laid Mrs. Lane in her grave."

"She was a fine woman," Jody said, a small smile of remembrance playing on her face. "She used to teach my Sunday school."

"Her boys used to help us out around the place," Mary said. "Big, fine boys, both of them."

"I didn't know she had any children, Miss Mary," Lou Ann said.

"That was back before your time, honey. Didn't either one of them come back from the war."

"This sure is nice fabric," Nancy said. "I can't seem to stop touching it."

"Know just exactly what you mean," Mary said. "Been walking around it and looking at it and playing with it ever since I got up."

Rooster was on her knees by the pile of brightly colored clothing. She lifted up one dress, made of printed fabric, with a high hand-knit collar and ruffled sleeves. It was a long dress, so long that when Rooster stood and held it to her body the hem almost touched the ground. The print was a simple one of tiny red roses, so many a dozen would barely cover the space of a child's palm, and even tinier pink hearts. It was the kind of print dress that was once sold in every general store in every small town in America, and today wasn't found outside of old-time movies and the attics of people who didn't ever like to throw things away.

And it was beautiful.

Rooster did a little swirl around, letting the full skirt billow out around her ankles. "Miss Mary, this is just adorable."

"Thank you, child," Mary replied, a small smile of memories playing on her lips.

"I don't remember ever seeing this before." Jody walked over and lifted the hem. The skirt was richly flounced and trimmed with the same hand-crocheted lace as the sleeves and neckline. "How old is this?"

"Older than any of you, I can tell you that

41

for sure," Mary replied. "I was married in that dress."

Jody let the hem drop. "And you're going to cut it up for a quilt?"

"I most certainly am. Can't imagine what on earth I was doing, holding on to that old thing for so long. Wasn't even sure I still had it. Found it down on the bottom of my hope chest. It was still wrapped in the same old paper I put it in, my goodness, it must be sixty years ago. Smelled of camphor and mothballs so bad I had to wash it six times. It's a wonder the thing's still in one piece."

"But, Momma," Jody searched for words. "This dress is priceless."

"It's in such good condition," Rooster said, lifting so as to inspect the dress more closely. "I can't believe it's so old."

Mary laughed, a short sound which showed her age. "I bought that dress at Jones' General Store. Back then, folks came from all

over the county to shop there. I can still remember crocheting the lace late at night, praying all the while I would make that man a good wife."

Lou Ann reached into the pile and came up with a beautiful blue satin dress. The body looked made for a large doll, but the skirt hung down a good four feet. "Miss Mary, what on earth is this?"

"What I spent all last night looking for," Mary replied. "That was the first nightie Jody's husband ever wore."

The ladies had a good laugh over that. Mary went on, "I learned this tradition from my own momma, God rest her soul. That's the way we used to dress up our children for their first look at the world."

"There's six of them here," Lou Ann said, sorting through the pile.

"That's right, honey. I had six children. Only two of them lived past their first year."

"I didn't know that, Momma," Jody said.

"Times change, child. Back then, there were lots of sicknesses just waiting to snatch the little ones away. All we had was a traveling country doctor and our prayers to see us through." Mary spent a long moment staring down at a beautiful pink gown, said quietly, "Sometimes it just wasn't enough."

"But you can't go cutting these up to make a quilt, Momma."

"Oh can't I?" Mary grasped the sides of her chair and pushed herself erect. "You just hand me those scissors over there on the ledge and watch what I can't do."

With a swiftness based on long experience Jody saw she had taken the wrong tack. She moved to Mary's side and tried again, "Momma, you've just got to let us help you with this."

Mary let herself be seated again. "I've been thinking about that too," she admitted.

"All the while I was rummaging around up-stairs and seeing just how tired this old body could get, I've been wondering how on earth I was going to get this quilt finished."

"We'd love to help you," Lou Ann ex-claimed.

"Sure to goodness would, Miss Mary," Nancy agreed.

"That's all well and good," Mary said. "And I'd be grateful, there's no question about that. But you're all gonna have to promise me one thing before you even think about picking up a needle."

"Anything," Jody said for them all. She looked at the wizened old lady sitting crouched over to one side in the big horsehair settee, saw the hands twisted up sideways with arthritis, and felt down in her heart the lady's incredible burden of years. A lump gathered so big in her throat she thought for a moment she was going to have to go get a drink of water.

"This is something the Lord's called me to do," Mary said in that quiet way of hers. "I can't explain it to you, but I know just as sure as I know my own name that this is something He wants done. And if I do it for Him, it's got to be the very best quilt I've ever made. Not a stitch out of place, not a piece of material laid wrong."

"We understand," Lou Ann said, caught up in the seriousness of the moment.

"There's something else. It came to me this morning as I was putting these things in the wash. For every stitch that goes into this quilt, I want you to say a prayer. And it can't be just any prayer. It has to be a prayer of thanksgiving."

A moment of silence greeted her words. Finally Jody said, with eyes warning her friends, "Why, that sounds just fine, Momma."

"Far too little thanks given these days," Mary said, more to herself than to the others. "With everything the Lord gives us, all we can think of is what we don't have. Like a bunch of spoiled children."

"We'd be happy to do that for you, Miss Mary," Lou Ann said, her eyes mirroring the blankness of Jody's.

"Not for me, child. Not for me. For our Lord. This is His quilt."

"Yes ma'am, that's what I meant."

"Then say what you mean," Mary said with a touch of sharpness. "I won't have a hand touch this quilt that doesn't have heart and mind fastened on their Father."

That pretty much put a stop to further talk. But as soon as they left, the talk bubbled back up like water from an underground spring. And that night the telephone lines near to melted from the heat.

"I just don't know what to think," Everett said to Jody over the phone. His brother Jonas never did talk enough to suit Everett when he was in one of his hyper moods. Talking to Jonas was like dropping a stone into a deep, dark well. You had to wait forever, and then there was only this distant plunk. Though he'd never admit it, Everett liked somebody to get all excited back at him, so he'd have a reason to do his little two-step and shout till his face got red.

Jody usually enjoyed Everett's little show. She knew it kept him from doing his song and dance in front of Lou Ann too often, and it always made her glad to have married the other brother. "It was awful funny looking at all those clothes laid out on the floor like that. I do believe I saw all her embroidered linens in that pile."

"I don't know, sister. I just don't know

what to think," Everett repeated, feeling the pressure rise. "Maybe it's time I went over and talked to the old folks home about a place for Momma."

That shocked Jody awake. Strange as Mary seemed over this quilt business, having her shipped off to some home was the furthest thing from Jody's mind. Jody opened her mouth, closed it, wondered how she could stop this before it went any further. "It's not as bad as all that, Ev."

Everett wasn't so easily slowed down. "Honey, maybe you don't see how she's slipping, living out near her and all. We oughtta have one of those specialists go out and give her a good check-up, listen to these stories of hers. Have her tell him about this call from heaven to make a quilt. At her age."

Jody had trouble answering right off, on account of her having this image flash inside her mind. It was one of those little things that didn't usually have any meaning since she saw it every day.

She saw herself standing at the kitchen sink, looking up the rise back behind their house as she did every morning while she was fixing breakfast. The sun was just clearing the woods behind her, throwing out that first golden beam. It caught Mary's white-work and turned it the color of molten gold. The rainwells Jonas had put in along the roof four or five years ago were galvanized and didn't need painting; when the sun hit them, they shone like a crown of light around her home. Jody stood there holding the phone and listening to Everett work himself up and saw herself looking out the window one dawn and knowing that someone else was living up there in Mary's home.

"Don't you dare call any doctor, you hear me?" The fury shocked even Jody. She swallowed, shook the vision from her mind, and said more quietly, "Don't go calling any doctor from the home, Everett."

She managed to cut the man off in midflow. He hesitated, said, "You sure, sister?"

"I'm sure." That strong no-nonsense tone she used with her children could be heard loud and clear. "I'll start making it a point to go up there every day and look in on her, help her out any way I can."

Everett's disappointment came through the phone. "I still think—"

"You just leave it with me, you hear what I'm saying? Mary'll be just fine where she is. She has all of us family to look after her." Before Everett could think up another protest, Jody said goodbye and set down the phone.

True to her word, Jody set off up the hill just as soon as the breakfast dishes were washed the next morning. But to her utter amazement, she heard Amy's bell-size laugh

ring out as she walked onto Mary's front stoop.

The women looked up as Jody entered the sitting room. "Why, good morning, child," said Mary. "What a nice surprise, two visitors so early on a morning."

Amy was sitting on the oval hook rug, the clothes from the pile spread out around her like a pastel rainbow. "I got to thinking about this last night and didn't think I'd ever get to sleep. I just couldn't wait to come out."

"Always nice to have company at a quilting," Mary said in her quiet way. "Just so long as you all remember to pray as you work."

"Momma—" The sight of three neatly folded white items lying there in front of Amy stopped Jody in mid-flow. In a shocked voice she asked, "Aren't those Poppa Joe's shirts?"

"His Sunday go-to-meeting shirts," Mary agreed. "Only things of his I kept. Found

them this morning when I was rummaging through his closet."

Jody turned round eyes toward Mary. "You're gonna use Poppa Joe's Sunday shirts in a quilt?"

"Can't imagine a better place for them," Mary said firmly. "That man prayed the better part of every Sunday in those shirts. I think he'd like the idea of seeing his church clothes being stitched up in a prayer quilt."

A prayer quilt. Despite herself, Jody had to admit that the words had a nice ring to them. A prayer quilt. She sat herself down in the other chair by the window to let it all sink in.

"Miss Mary was just telling me about when the children were still young," said Amy.

"It came to me this morning," Mary said. "Strange how something that happened over forty years ago can look clearer to my mind than what I had for breakfast this morning. I was laying out those shirts there and recalled how Jonas," she stopped to give Jody her memory-laden smile. "I mean my husband, honey, not my boy.

"Every Sunday we'd walk back up the rise from church, and before he'd go into the house Jonas would always stop by the well. We had running water even back then. First house in the county to put in inside water. Jonas had the man come by and drill down beside the well; then he laid copper piping to the kitchen. But he always said the water never tasted as nice out of the pipe as it did straight from the well."

Mary's eyes misted over as she looked out in front of her and saw what was meant for her eyes alone. "He'd haul the bucket up on that worn rope. I was after him till the day he died to put another rope on. Someday that rope was going to break and then he'd have the dickens of a time trying to fish it out. That well must have been all of eighty feet deep. But he'd just smile that slow smile of his, and tell me there wasn't anybody interested in that well but him, and he liked the way that old rope fitted to his hand."

Mary paused to wipe her mouth with an age-spotted hand, then went on, "Everett was always right there beside Poppa Joe, screaming to be picked up so he could drink too. Jonas had this way of drinking that just seemed to go on forever, stopping to breathe that long sigh between each draught. Like to have drove that boy crazy, having to wait till Poppa was finished before he'd pick Everett up and let him drink too."

For some reason Jody saw her own children, had a little kaleidoscope of images all crowding there in front of her eyes. She saw the little things that touched her heart so, and tried to imagine what it would be like to look back in thirty years and realize that all those special times were over forever. Over and gone, yet even when they were there the strains and pressures of the moment often washed all the joy away.

"A lot to be thankful for," Mary said softly, her eyes focusing on the room once more. She turned and smiled a sad, sweet smile for Jody. "The Lord's been awful good to me."

"Good to all of us," Jody said, though she had a little trouble getting the words out.

"That's the truth," Amy said from her place on the floor, her eyes a little misty too.

"And that's what we're here for, isn't it," Mary said, her voice gathering strength. "We're going to sit here and thank Him for all these wonders. Every cut, every stitch, every piece we lay down, each one's going to have its own little prayer to help set it in place. Doesn't matter if this thing takes us twenty years. That's the way it's going to be."

"It was a real strange feeling," Jody told her husband that night. "I got down on the floor and started cutting and felt, I don't know, kinda uncomfortable at first sitting there with my scissors, trying to cut straight and pray at the same time. I couldn't think of anything to say. And I sure as goodness couldn't look Amy in the eyes. I was sure if I did I'd break out laughing, it felt so funny."

Jody had a way of talking to her husband that was born of long years of talking as much to herself as to him. Jonas was such a quiet man. He'd sit for as long as she held him with her voice, the dinner dishes piled up where their oldest boy had sat, the kids upstairs raising Cain, all excited because they had been freed from their usual routine of kitchen chores. Whenever Jody had something to talk

to Jonas about, she sent them upstairs with the promise that if they weren't quiet she'd be up soon enough to put them to bed. But they'd learned long ago that if they gave the elders twenty minutes of relative calm to get deep in discussion, they could peel the tiles off the roof without much worry.

Jonas was a carver. It was his only real hobby, and he tried to spend at least an hour or so at it every evening. When the house was quiet and the kids in bed, he'd pull his little tray out from under his favorite chair and sit and carve. Sometimes it was soap, sometimes sandalwood, sometimes just a likely-looking stick he'd picked up on the way home. The first gift he'd ever presented to Jody, back when they had just started courting, was a lovely little soapstone jewel box. What's this, she had asked him at the time. Jonas had replied, seeing as how you're going to carry my heart around with you, I thought you might

need something to put it in.

He had all of these tiny instruments, some made for carvers and some coming from a jeweller friend who was always after Jonas to let him sell the pieces. Every time the jeweller was over he walked around picking them up and inspecting them and shaking his head. What on earth are you doing, he'd ask Jonas, letting the kids play with these things? Jonas replied with an easy smile that looked so much like Mary's and the words, just letting my children enjoy them the only way they know how.

Whenever Jody sent the children off and started on one of her evening talks, Jonas would walk into the living room and come back with his carving tray. He might look up once during the whole time she talked. He just sat there, his face set in those calm expressionless lines, and carved. It amazed Jody how those big, hard hands could be so gentle, so careful, so patient, and so gifted.

When she was younger she used to try and force a reaction out of him, ask him direct questions and badger him, always trying to draw him out of that placid shell. The last time she tried it was the year before their first child was born. She lost her temper a bit, frustrated by his eternal calm, and half-shouted that she could just as well read the telephone book out loud to him as talk about something really important. Jonas looked up at that and said the first words he'd spoken that evening. That's just not true, he said, and the calm force behind those words startled her. But you never say anything, Jody told him. I've never been a man with much to say, Jonas replied. Jody asked, well, do you want me to stop talking and be quiet too? As long as you want to talk, Jonas replied, I want to listen. I love the sound of your voice, and the sound of your heart coming out with the words.

Jody had long since grown accustomed to talking to her silent man, and had made two interesting discoveries along life's road. The first was that a silent listener like Jonas could draw her deepest thoughts out better than the world's best talker. It was at times like these, when she had said something from the deepest part of herself or spoken out a revelation which came from somewhere else, that Jonas would look up at her and smile what Jody had always thought of as Mary's smile.

The second thing she discovered was that not only did Jonas really listen, he remembered. He would come to her, days and sometimes even weeks later, and mention something she had said in one of these talks. She would spend a couple of frantic minutes searching her memory for what he was referring to, then spend a good while afterward thanking the Lord for giving her such a man.

That night Jonas was working on one of

his little men, a gift for their daughter. She had a veritable army of tiny friends, each one about the size of her six-year-old hand. They remained lined up on her dresser until time came for tea parties and long afternoon chats. Jonas's jeweller friend refused to go into their daughter's room at all. He said looking at all those little fellers going to waste up there gave him indigestion.

Jonas had the tray set in the place where his dinner plate had been, his sleeves rolled up to expose wiry arms, and those big work-strong hands wrapped around a little steel carving hook. He'd pick a couple of times, blow, inspect, flick at the spot with a tiny smidgen of sanding paper, pick some more. And listen. Jody had long since learned that he always, always listened.

"But you know, this praying while we worked was something real important to Mary," Jody told her husband. "I could tell.

She stopped every now and then and read from that big old Bible, then go back and cut some more. And the way she did it, honey, it was like something out of a slow-motion picture. She'd cut just like this." Jody made sure Jonas lifted his eyes before cutting the air in excruciating slowness. "I couldn't watch her for long, it just drove me crazy. You know how I am, there's so much to get done and so little time, I swear I don't even know what I'm doing up there at the house with so much to do around here."

Jody bent her own head and started making little slow-motion designs on the tabletop with one finger. "I don't know how long I was up there, but after a while all that stuff just stopped mattering. I don't know as I can explain it, but it was like everything just slowed down. All the things I've been worrying about, Timmy's problems at school and the car and the chores, it just went away."

Jody lifted both hands and pressed against her forehead as though trying to squeeze the memory clear. "I was thinking about when Betty was little and got so sick, and how the doctor said he wasn't sure she'd get over it, and how tired we both were when she started getting better, you remember?"

"I remember," Jonas said softly.

Jody raised her head and was surprised to find him sitting there and watching her full on, the carving and the tools set aside. She couldn't ever recall having seen that before.

She collected herself and went on, "So I just started thanking God for healing our little girl. I started to apologize for not having said it sooner, and then stopped myself, you know, because Mary said we weren't supposed to say anything but thanks. So I thanked Him for quite a while. I think it was right about then that it started feeling like time was slowing down."

Jonas nodded as though he understood, just a tiny nod, but a nod just the same. His expression didn't change, it almost never did. But his attention was focused on her with an almost frightening intensity.

"We were laying out the patterns, trying to get the colors to match. We're going to do a flower design, with a central circle and fourteen petals coming out. And you know, whenever I've done a quilt with others before, there's always been a lot of talk and comparison and gossip, argument too. Everybody has their own idea of how they want the pattern laid out." Jody found that the intensity of Jonas's gaze somehow made the memory come alive for her once again. "But this time, honey, there wasn't even any talk. We just laid it out as we wanted, almost in turn, and I really think every one of us was praying as we did it. I know I was.

"Then the next thing I knew, I looked at

the clock on her mantel, and I'd been sitting there for almost four hours. When I got home the children had already made their own lunch and gone out to play."

Jonas looked at her for a long moment, then picked up his carving tool and rolled it back and forth between his scarred thumb and forefinger.

"I think you oughtta go back and help out as much as you can," he said to Jody.

"There was something else," Jody added. "All the rest of today I've been thinking of things I want to go back and give thanks for. Everywhere I turn it seems like I'm looking at things that I've spent years taking for granted, and now they're all coming alive again. I might sound crazy, but even the kids seem more important—no, not that. More beautiful. No, not beautiful."

"Jody," Jonas said in his quiet, strong way.

"I don't know how to, wait, I know. It's

like, when I stop and thank Him, I'm really seeing it for the first time. Not like I've never seen it before, but like I've never seen it with His eyes before. Everything becomes a gift then." She looked up. "Does that make any sense?"

"I want you to go up and help out Momma whenever you can," Jonas repeated.

"I was planning to," Jody said. "I really think there's something special going on up there."

There is a lot of work that goes into a handmade quilt, long before the first stitch is ever sewn. Once the backing is stretched across the frame and the front piece is chosen and the design is selected and the various bits of cloth are all brought out and washed till they're limp as used paper towels, once the measuring's been done a dozen times, once the design's cut out one time for all the other designs to be compared to, once the little sheaves of fabric are all scissored and trimmed a second time, once they've been mixed and matched a thousand times until all the colors are just as they should be, once the designs are laid out across the floor with one extra set put aside for covering the mistakes that are bound to happen, once the design pattern has been measured and drawn and cut from the front fabric, then and only then can the stitching begin. And as any good quilt-maker will tell you, the work doesn't really get under way until it's time to pick up the needle.

When Everett arrived five days later for his regular Wednesday visit, there were three ladies cutting out petals, one doing the inner circles, two busy drawing out the design on the front fabric, and another helping his mother stretch and pull and separate and flatten all the strands of cotton batting.

And what's more, the place was as still as a church bowed in silent prayer.

Everett stood on the front stoop and peered through the screen door, not sure he belonged, and feeling truly riled over a bunch of strange women upsetting his routine. He pushed his hat back so as to be able to scratch the front of his balding head, and pressed his face up against the screen like a little boy watching his mother bake pies on a Saturday afternoon.

Without warning, one of the women started singing, softly at first, "What a Friend We Have in Jesus." Before she was halfway through the first stanza, the whole room was rocking to the sound of that old-time hymn.

At the sound of all those voices Everett

suddenly felt the outsider, the one who didn't belong. A big hole opened up about heart-level, and Everett turned and started scuffling off the porch.

"That you, son?" Everett turned to find Mary at the door.

"Momma?" It startled him, seeing her through the screen. It was somehow like Mary had dropped thirty years, her gentle features losing all their wrinkles and turning the clock back to when he was a little boy.

Mary pushed the screen aside, and Everett felt his heart slow down as the old woman appeared in the natural light.

"Come on in, son. I doubt the coffee's much good, I was up so early this morning. Maybe I ought to make another pot."

"I just brewed some up fresh, Miss Mary," said a voice from inside. "Hope that's all right."

"Well, bless you, child. I know Everett'll be pleased."

But Everett wasn't sure how he felt about it all as he let Mary take his arm and lead him into the crowded sitting room. "Y'all know my boy, don't you?"

There was a chorus of yes ma'ams and a lot of sheepish smiles, like a group of little girls caught playing in their mother's closet.

"Ladies," Everett mumbled, feeling totally out of place. "Momma, maybe it'd be better if I came back another day."

"Don't talk nonsense." Mary led her younger boy through the doorway and down the little connecting hall to the big country kitchen. "Now you just sit yourself down right there at the table and I'll pour you a cup and we'll chat. Those ladies can take care of themselves for a spell."

Mary eased herself down into the chair opposite him, and lovingly guided her boy toward forgetting the women in the next room and the worries he had with his work and the problems he'd been carrying all his life. Every man needed the chance to set down his guard from time to time, she'd always told anybody who'd listen. The problem was, most men got so used to working in a world that called for invisible armor all the time, they forgot they were even wearing it.

Once he was talking without thinking, Mary allowed herself to relax a little and just love her boy. Everett had always held a special place in her heart. Jonas, her elder surviving son, was so much like his father it was uncanny—big and hale and quiet and solid. Jonas was not somebody who needed very much. Everett, poor little Everett, he'd been a sickly child. And too many of his younger years had been spent standing in the shadow of his big brother.

While Jonas had grown up strong and

solid as a barn door, Everett had grown out. Mary always looked at Everett's pudgy round face and fat arms and protruding belly and saw the little lonely sensitive child that needed an extra padding of protection around a heart that broke too easily for this world.

She watched her Everett grow up into a young man who tried hard as he could to be one of the boys, and even when they had accepted him as one of their own, Everett had never known happiness. He'd grown up letting the others of his age mold his character and his behavior, and it seemed like only Mary could see the yearning in those sad little eyes.

"Your wife was here again yesterday," Mary told him. "She's a darling woman, Everett. I've always thought of her as the little girl I didn't have."

Everett's pudgy features lit up at the mention of Lou Ann. "You never told me that, Momma."

"Never told you a lot of things. It's true just the same."

As she spoke, Mary recalled something Lou Ann had said the previous afternoon as she was leaving. The two women had been cleaning up after all the others had left, when suddenly Lou Ann had said, I've never thanked you for Everett, have I? Something in the way she'd said it brought tears to Mary's eyes. I was so scared when Everett brought you home that first time, Mary had replied. There was so much need in that boy, I was scared to death he'd gone out and found somebody who'd never understand. Lou Ann had smiled at her and said, I knew you were worried. That's why I wasn't concerned over how cross you were with me. Anybody with eyes could see that Everett was your favorite. Mary had laughed to cover how

touched she was by the words. He just needed me more than anybody else, I suppose, Mary had replied. Who'd have thought there was all that goodness just waiting to come out, Lou Ann had said. Child, Mary had told her, if it had been a lesser woman than you, that goodness would have never existed. It took a woman with a heart of gold to make that boy come alive.

Goodness there may have been in Everett, but it was not something many could see at first glance. Everett was not a pretty man, and age did not sit well on him. His formerly sandy-blond hair now looked like a hard rain had rinsed all the color out. His hair was not turning white so much as it was becoming transparent. Everett's chin tended to disappear nowadays into little layers of sagginess when he lowered his head. His face blotched into shades of pink and red when he got excited, and he had the deep, gasping cough of a formerly consumptive child. People who knew him well said Everett was a good man, he just tried too hard. His laugh was forced, his good-old-boy style too jovial, the fear in his eyes there for all to see.

Everett spooned sugar into his coffee and said to Mary, "I still don't see what's possessed you to get started with another doggone quilt, Momma."

"There's not a thing in this world that's going to disturb our Wednesday mornings, son," Mary replied, understanding him perfectly. "Now you just put those ladies in the other room out of your head and tell me about the family."

Everett hid his embarrassment behind a loud slurp of coffee. His mother's ability to see right through him had always left him feeling downright exposed. "You didn't answer my question, Momma."

"The Lord's shown me what He wants

just as clearly as He can, son."

"What, He came down and spoke from the burning bush?" Everett gave a little high-pitched chuckle at his own cleverness. "Lit up one of the magnolias in your front yard?"

Sometimes after her visits with Everett, Mary would look back and wonder that the well of patience did not run dry. Mary looked down at her hands, rubbed them back and forth, one upon the other. Her voice had that quiet warning to it when she spoke. "There's not a soul on this earth who knows how many days they've got left. Not you, not me, not any of the ladies sitting there in the front room. All we can hope for is that what time we have is spent as the Lord wants us to."

Mary looked up and fastened her son with a strong gaze. "I won't say this again, Everett. The Lord has told me that I am to make Him a quilt, and it is to be sewn together with

77

prayers. That is all there is to be said about it, do you hear me?"

"I hear you," Everett replied sullenly. "Can't say as I understand it, though, a lady of your age starting another quilt."

"I didn't say we'd always understand what the Lord intends for us, now, did I." Mary pointed to the windowsill, said, "Reach over there for the little Bible, son."

Everett turned around, saw between the hanging plants a little New Testament covered in wood from an olive tree. The sight startled him. He lifted the tiny book, and recalled a six-year-old boy who saved his pennies for a whole summer, then sent off to the mail-order company for a Bible bound in olive wood from the Holy Land. It was the first Christmas present he had ever paid for with his own money.

He had to clear his throat before he could

say, "I didn't know you still had this, Momma."

"Can't read it anymore," Mary replied. "The print's just a blur. But I like to have it around me. Reminds me of a little boy I loved to distraction. Still do, for that matter."

Everett kept his eyes on the small book as he rubbed his hands over the smooth polished surface and recalled the excitement of a Christmas morning long ago. The joy over his own presents had paled in comparison to how he had looked forward to his momma opening that gift brought all the way from Israel.

"Can you read that little print, son?"

" 'Course I can."

"Open it up to Romans, please, sir." Mary closed her eyes, thought a moment, said, "Romans, chapter one, verse twenty-one. Read it to me, if you please."

Everett searched, turning the fragile

pages with fingers that seemed too big and clumsy for the little volume. He read, " 'For although they knew God, they neither glorified him as God nor gave thanks to him, but their thinking became futile and their foolish hearts were darkened.' "

" 'Nor gave thanks to him,' " Mary repeated. "Isn't that something. We're not just talking about some little act we can take on when times are good and there's a few extra minutes lying about. Paul says just plain as the nose on your face that this is one of the most basic responsibilities we have. We must glorify our God and we must give thanks to Him. All the sins and all the confusion that Paul talks about for the rest of that chapter stem from people not doing those two things.

"I've been sitting up here growing old and watching the world speed up, faster and faster, until I can hardly believe people don't get dizzy just standing still. And when they come up to see me, all they can talk about is how much they've got to get done. Seems to me like they work themselves toward an early grave just so tomorrow they can rest a spell."

Mary leaned closer. "Son, let me tell you a little secret I've learned in these long years of mine. Tomorrow never comes. You either have it today, or you don't."

She waved her hand around to take in the room. "I'm not talking about possessions. I'm talking about what counts. The things of the Spirit. Love, patience, kindness, compassion. And a thankful heart. A body's got to take time each and every day to thank their Lord for all that's theirs. Plain and simple, son. It's got to start today, no matter how busy you are, nor how much is still left undone, nor how many problems are piled up on your head and heart. Giving thanks is one thing that can't wait.

"The night I realized the Lord wanted me

to make this quilt, I asked myself, now what business does an old lady like me have in taking on something like this? It wasn't until the next morning, when I was sitting there listening to the newsman talk about some disaster or something, that I realized. Came to me clear as day. It's a lesson that's been forgotten, the importance of giving thanks. And if I can help one person see how necessary it is with this work, why, the Lord's will has been done. Doesn't matter a whit, that quilt being finished. What's important is those ladies in there remembering what it's like to be really and truly grateful to their Lord."

It was two days later, early enough in the morning for the ladies to have cut a dark swathe across the dew-covered lawn as they arrived. The sitting room smelled of coffee and baking bread, and was surprisingly silent for the number of people sitting on chairs, floor, and footstools. A couple were humming, one was staring out into space with a little smile on her face, and three were on their hands and knees around Mary's chair as they discussed the color-coding in whispers. The room's stillness was too precious a gift to be disturbed with loud voices and unnecessary chatter.

Lou Ann raised herself up from the tiny space behind the television and walked over to Mary. In her hands was a parchment-colored sheet of brittle paper.

"Miss Mary, did you write this?"

Mary looked up from the myriad of triangular fabrics in her lap. "What have you got there, sister?"

Lou Ann held out the sheet, said, "Did

you use to write poetry, Miss Mary?"

Mary took the paper and examined it. A tremor seemed to pass over her body. "Land sakes," she whispered.

Lou Ann bent nearer. "You've gone all white, Miss Mary. Are you all right?"

Mary looked up, said in a fragile voice, "Where on earth did you find this?"

Lou Ann made a frightened little gesture back behind her. "I was just looking through your old Bibles, Miss Mary. I was reading the passages you had marked, you know, just turning the pages, and I found this sheet." She gave the old woman a very worried look. "I'm real sorry if I shouldn't have done it. Are you all right?"

"Everything's just fine, child," Mary said quietly and turned away from a roomful of watching faces. She stared out the window a long time, long enough for worried glances to be passed back and forth among her guests.

Mary turned back, saw that Lou Ann really was concerned, smiled with the warmth that was all her own and patted the stool beside her chair. "Sit down here for a moment, honey, and I'll tell you why it gave me such a start."

"I'm really sorry, Miss Mary. It was just so beautiful and I thought—"

"Shush, honey, there's nothing wrong with what you've done. It just startled me. I haven't seen this in, oh, I don't know how many years. Not since before Everett was born."

When Lou Ann was settled Mary went on, "Between Jonas and Everett I had three other babies. The first two were stillborn, God rest their little souls. The third was my only little girl. She was the smilingest little baby you ever saw. That's about all I can remember about her now, that and the way she would follow me with her eyes all over the room. I

know it's not possible, no baby a month old can do it, but that's the way it was. Got no reason to fib about it, now, do I. I would walk into the room and her little face would just light up like a candle. She'd lie there too tiny to move anything more than her head, and she'd follow me with her eyes no matter where I went. And if I went out and came back in again, that little darling was still watching the door. Soon as she saw me she'd smile again. Happiest baby I ever did see. Hardly ever cried, and if she did all I had to do was pick her up and she'd settle right down. Little angel was all she was."

Mary sighed long and soft, shook her head, "Came in one morning when she was just four months old and found her lying there dead. Crib death, the doctor told me. Nothing anybody could have done about it. Like to have torn me apart, losing my little girl. Didn't know a body could stand that

86

much grief and still survive."

The room was so silent that the mocking-bird outside the sitting room window sounded jarringly loud. All eyes watched Mary turn and stare out the window, hiding the emotions that etched the ancient face, searching the sunlit lawn for a smiling little girl.

"Dr. Caswell was preacher then," Mary went on, her face still pointed toward the window. "None of you would remember him, but there was a fine man. A *good* man. Never afraid to share a body's burdens. Don't know what would have happened to me if it wasn't for him. One time he came by, I suppose it must have been a few months after the funeral, Dr. Caswell gave me that sheet there and told me the story of George Matheson. Have any of you ladies ever heard of him?"

There was a chorus of no ma'ams about the room as work was forgotten, tools laid aside, bodies settled to more comfortable positions.

"George Matheson was a man of the Lord, born and raised in Scotland. I forget when he lived, but I know it wasn't in this century. He fell in love with a beautiful young lady, and they planned to marry. Not long before his wedding day, George Matheson discovered he was going blind."

Mary waited until the room quietened, then continued, "He did what he had to do, went to his young lady and told her the news. Told her she could break off the engagement if she wanted, but that he still loved her and wanted to marry if she would have him. The woman thought about it for several days, then came back and said that though she loved him, she did not want to spend the rest of her life with a blind man. And the wedding was off. Soon after this, George Matheson wrote a hymn."

Mary turned back from the window. She lifted the brittle page with trembling hands, looked at it for a long moment, then handed it over to Lou Ann. Her voice was as shaky as her hands when she said, "Read that first verse for me, honey, my eyes aren't what they used to be."

Lou Ann studied the ancient script, read in a halting voice,

> O Love that wilt not let me go,
> I rest my weary soul in Thee;
> I give Thee back the life I owe,
> That in Thine ocean depths its flow
> May richer, fuller be.

"The Lord holds me always in His love, Dr. Caswell told me," Mary said to the silent room. "Always there, always loving, always giving, always healing. At my weakest, the Lord is strongest."

Mary paused a moment, kneading one

hand with the other, then said, "George Matheson went blind, and he didn't marry the girl. He lived a full life for his Lord, and toward the end of his time on earth he wrote a prayer. I think more than anything these words were what saw me through my own dark times." She looked at Lou Ann, said, "Just read that section there at the bottom that starts, 'My God,' please child."

Lou Ann cleared her throat, wiped her eyes, read,

My God,
I have never thanked thee for my thorn.
I have thanked thee a thousand times
    for my roses,
But never once for my thorn.
Teach me the glory of my cross,
Teach me the value of my thorn.
Show me that I have climbed to thee
    by the path of my pain.

90

Show me that my tears have made
    my rainbows.

"There's lessons right along to the end of
the road," Mary said, her eyes back on the
window. She sighed, shook her head, said
softly to the world outside, "What *strength*
that man must have had."

Pretty soon the whole town was talking
about the quilt, give or take a few souls who
didn't think the whole mess amounted to a
hill of beans on a hot day. The regular crew
was singled out for talk and gossip, the opin-
ions varying according to personalities. For
some it was a curious thing, how grown-up
women with jobs and families could see fit to
spend so much time on a silly old quilt. Oth-

ers thought it a Christian duty, helping poor Miss Mary out on something she had no business starting in the first place. Then there were some who heard of the praying and the Bible reading and the singing, but they weren't really sure they could believe it all. Others listened and nodded and wished in silence they had the courage and the time to go up and join the group.

When asked, those who went were usually very excited about it, yet bashful at the same time. It was hard to describe, the communion and the joy and the stillness they found in the little house on the hill.

Some of those who went regularly stopped saying much when asked about it, or at least stopped opening their hearts every time someone asked them how the quilt was getting on. It was hard to face those frozen little know-it-all smiles, those calculating, cold eyes beneath carefully set coiffures, that unspoken desire to probe for weakness and fault and something to criticize. So the women often did what they felt they had to, which was develop a little two-sentence piece that started out with how marvelous it was to take time for prayer every day and ended with how the lady ought to come up and join them. And the lady would cover her disappointment at not gaining anything else for her rumor-mill with another little cold-eyed smile, and say the inevitable, Miss Mary is such a beautiful woman, and change the subject.

The morning sessions in Mary's sitting room took on the sort of established routine that was possible only when people did what they needed to do because they wanted to. The first ladies to arrive each morning made coffee and set out the various scissors and measuring tapes and sewing baskets. If a pie or coffee cake was brought, it was put in the oven and the temperature set on low. Bread dough was placed on the counter to rise and covered with a damp cloth. The women chatted with Mary and marked out the work completed the day before and laughed quite a lot. There was a sense of anticipation in the room, a feeling that the little girl inside each of them was let loose to laugh and chase sunbeams and share a little of the joy they thought locked away forever.

Most mornings the ladies would only stay an hour and then hurry back to what they had come to call the outside world. Mary would see them off the way she greeted them, with a soft smile and a blessing and a few words to show how wonderful it was to have them stop by. The ladies would always hesitate by the door, feeling pushed to go, regretting that they were leaving, and sort of wondering down deep if maybe that push they were feeling to depart was not truly as urgent as they made it out to be.

Every few minutes, Mary would remind them of their purpose, their responsibility to say a prayer of thanks with each stitch sewn. It doesn't matter if this quilt takes another twenty years, Mary would say a dozen times a day. What is important is that we all, each and every one of us, remember what it's like to be grateful.

That morning Jody waited until the room was pretty full, then said she had something she wanted to talk about. She found she couldn't address the room directly. With a shyness she hadn't known for years, she turned to Mary and talked, though her words were meant for all the room.

"I found the prettiest Bible passage last night, Momma," Jody said.

Lately Mary had been spending more and more time just sitting and looking out the window, the work lying unattended in her lap. She turned at the sound of her name, blinked a few times as though not remembering where she was or why the people were there, said, "What's that, child?"

"A Bible passage I found last night," Jody said, feeling somehow very young and very embarrassed.

"Isn't that nice," Mary said, bringing the room into focus with her smile. "Why don't you read it for us."

"Yes, ma'am." Jody opened her Bible, said, "It's from the hundredth Psalm."

Enter his gates with thanksgiving
    and his courts with praise;
    give thanks to him and praise his name.
For the Lord is good and his love
    endures forever;
    his faithfulness continues through
    all generations.

"I've always loved that passage," Mary

said, nodding her head very slowly, as though the effort was almost too much for her. "Why don't you tell us how that spoke to your heart?"

"Well," Jody said, patting at wayward hair with movements made jerky by her nervousness. "I just read it and kind of saw myself walking into the presence of the Lord, like it says. And the way I could do it was by praising His name."

She made a little gesture as if she were trying to grab words out of the air, searching to find a way to say it so that the emotion she had felt would live for the others. "It was so beautiful there, with this love and light and everything. And I saw how all the things that I worried about were shadows that kept me from seeing what I really needed to do, which was be thankful."

Mary waited until she was sure Jody was finished, and said softly, "Child, you don't

97

know how those words make me feel."

With visible effort Mary rose to her feet, and the room saw that the lady could not stand upright. She leaned over slightly, her right arm bent up like a broken chicken wing. She held it close to her side, pressing in to keep some unseen pain from escaping and submerging her. And those in the room felt their hearts stand still.

Jody was up and beside her before Mary could take her first step. "Momma, what's the matter?"

"Be an angel and help me back to the bedroom," Mary said.

"Can we get you something?" Lou Ann asked.

"Not a thing, thank you. You just sit there and think on what this child has told you." Mary let herself be half-led, half-carried through the silent room. When she was in the doorway leading to the back hall she turned and said to them all, "And finish what you've started."

That afternoon Mary had not risen from her bed, and her color did not look good, so Jody decided it was time to listen to sense and not to Mary's protests. She called the doctor, and when he heard who it was he promised to stop by on his way home.

Dr. Horace Martin had the sort of bedside manner that made most people want to get well just to make him happy. And those who couldn't will themselves well were grateful for his care. His eyes held the light of somebody who was just waiting to hear the punchline of a really good joke, and even on the coldest days his hands somehow stayed

warm. He had forgotten more secrets than most people ever knew, and came close to matching the minister for hearing out people's troubles.

But his face was serious and his eyes grave when he finished Mary's examination. He folded up his stethoscope and put it back into his little black bag before saying, "Miss Mary, I think maybe I oughtta call us a car to take you over to the hospital."

Jody felt that little cloud of fear that had been hovering around her all day densify into a solid lump of ice that settled in her belly. She reached out and grasped the doorjamb for support.

Mary did not need to raise her voice to get the message across. "Horace Martin, you are going to do no such thing."

"It's just a few tests, Miss Mary, there's nothing—"

"Don't be silly, young man." Her voice

was barely above a whisper, but her gaze still brooked no back talk. "What on earth do I need tests for? I'm old and I'm sick. There. I've just saved us both a lot of trouble."

Dr. Horace Martin knew Mary well enough to quit while he was able. He gave her hand a little pat, smiled in defeat, stood, and signaled for Jody and Lou Ann to follow him out.

Once the door was closed, Jody had to fight to keep her voice steady as she asked, "Is she going to be all right?"

There were some things that Horace Martin had never become comfortable with. His eyes said one thing while his voice said another. "She's old but she's strong. Why don't we give her a couple of days and see how it develops."

Jody was too numb to wring her hands. "Should I try to talk her into going to the hospital?"

It showed the kind of man Dr. Horace Martin truly was when he fought down his first reaction and said instead, "Maybe the best thing for her right now is to stay where she's most comfortable."

By mid-morning of the next day, Mary's front sitting room was jammed. Lou Ann had been there since letting the kids off at school, granting Jody a chance to go home and get a few hours sleep. Voices were even more hushed than usual.

Just before lunch Lou Ann went back to find Mary's eyes open. "Are you all right, Momma? Can I get you something to eat?"

Mary motioned toward the glass on her bedstead. When Lou Ann had helped her drink, she asked, "Are they working on my quilt?"

The question caught Lou Ann by surprise. "Why, yes, ma'am, that is—"

"You march right back out there and tell them to remember what I said." Mary's voice carried surprising strength for being so soft. "Not a stitch is to be sewn without a prayer of thanks."

"Yes, Momma, I will. But don't you want—"

"Right this instant, young lady," Mary said, and set her mouth in firm lines. When Lou Ann was by the door she added, "And you might just call Preacher Louis and ask him to stop by sometime."

Preacher Louis was a wisp of a man with the voice of a hurricane, rolling and thundering and shaking the rafters. People who'd never seen him preach wondered how such a small weak-looking man with watery gray eyes could ride herd on such a large congregation. The question was never voiced by anyone who'd sat through a Sunday morning with Preacher Louis. As one old-timer put it, there was no question where the power came from. Up at the altar, the man burned like a freshly-lit Coleman cooking stove.

The sitting room was still full of ladies that evening when the preacher arrived. Outside in the twilight a cluster of husbands and older children were talking in the low voices of people accustomed to the gatherings of a death watch. Preacher Louis greeted the men with his mild voice, commented on how warm the evening had remained, and pushed his way through the screen door. He stopped on the threshold and stared over the silent group with gentle gray eyes showing surprise. Women intent on work raised their heads to the reverend and offered greetings, but little was said and less time lost as they continued with their slow, careful stitching.

Jody and Lou Ann came up together. The reverend looked at them, said, "Don't these ladies have families waiting?"

"We've been trying to get them to go home for almost four hours now," Jody said. "They'll leave for a little while and then sneak back in."

"Lynn told me straight out that if I locked the door she'd break in a window," Lou Ann said.

"I would, too," Lynn affirmed from her place by the frame. "Miss Mary told us to finish this and that's exactly what we're going to do."

"Tell her we're not forgetting the prayers, Reverend," Amy said from where she was finishing up her own circular pattern.

"Yes, well, perhaps I'd best speak to Miss Mary." Preacher Louis allowed himself to be led through the women and down the back hallway to the bedroom. He smiled his thanks to Jody and Lou Ann and shut the door in their faces.

More than an hour passed before the minister reappeared. He went with Jody and Lou Ann into the kitchen, refused their offer of coffee, spent a long moment tracing the pattern in the tablecloth.

"Might as well say it, Reverend," Lou Ann said, blinking at tears. "It's clear enough in your face."

Reverend Louis raised his eyes, studied the two faces carefully before smiling his thin little smile and saying, "That is one beautiful lady."

"What did she say?" Jody pressed.

"Miss Mary told me it was time she was going home," Reverend Louis replied.

When Jody could talk again, she said, "O dear sweet Lord."

"Said it like she was talking about the

price of eggs," Reverend Louis said. "She had a message for you two, said I was to wait but I think maybe I'll tell you now. She said for you both to be strong."

Work on the quilt became a twenty-four-hour affair. Ladies whose husbands worked the night shift would come by for an hour or so, only to find a few others who just couldn't sleep and thought maybe they'd stop in and keep Jody or Lou Ann or Jonas company. Nobody noticed Everett. He had come in not long after the preacher had left and had not moved since. He remained camped out in the chair beside Mary's bed, not saying anything except when he read to her. He slept in little snatches when his eyes wouldn't stay open anymore, the Bible open in his lap in case Mary woke and wanted to hear something. As soon as she closed her eyes again, though, he'd stop his reading and just sit there and watch her.

When Jonas came in the first time, he'd started to ask his brother to leave them alone for a moment, but when he saw the look in Everett's eyes he just didn't have the heart to say anything. Lou Ann brought Everett food every once in a while, then stood over him to make sure he ate.

Just before dawn on the fifth day after Preacher Louis's visit, the last stitch was made. Seven tired ladies stepped back from the upright frame and looked with pleased expressions on their work.

It was a glorious quilt.

The outer edges were framed in shiny swatches of multicolored satin. They gave way to a stretch of pastel blue as clear and soft as the morning sky. And against this background were set the circular flower-patterns. Radiating out from each inner circle were fourteen petals, and each pattern was made from four different materials, four different printed designs.

Somehow the different colors and designs and prints melted together and formed a new, larger pattern. The older ladies who had done quilts before knew this was the key. If the patterns were in true harmony they were seen yet not seen, like each brushstroke of a painting was not seen separately from the whole.

The quilt was a picture and a story. It was a testimony to a time when pressures did not cry out for urgent things to be constantly tended to, when the world had not created a thousand different temptations pulling free time into a myriad of mindless activities. It told of values and patience and timeless meanings. It drew the person in. It spoke of comfort and rest. It soothed with the gentleness of a mother's kiss.

Jonas arrived with the sun, bringing the doctor for his morning visit. The two men stopped in front of the upright frame as though drawn to the spot.

"That is a work of art," Dr. Martin said. "You ladies should be proud of yourselves."

"Too tired to be proud," Jody said, smiling at her husband.

"I'm not," Amy said. "I'm so proud I could burst."

"I want to take that frame apart and put it back together in Mary's room," Jonas decided. "Want her to see it just like this."

"You better wait till Lou Ann gets here," Jody said. "She'd skin you alive if she wasn't here to watch Momma's face."

"You get busy with that, then," Dr. Martin said. "I'll go see to our patient. Everett still in there?"

"Hasn't moved in five days," Jody said, the light in her eyes dimming. "I went in a couple of hours ago and covered him with a blanket. Momma seemed to be resting comfortably."

It took them the better part of the morning to unfasten the quilt, take the screws out of the frame's corners, and set it up again in Mary's room. They had to wait until they were sure she was asleep before starting to rebuild it. While they worked they kept shooting little glances at each other, raising up a little and looking at the bed, half-grinning at the thought of what Mary would say, making a lot of noise in a quiet sort of way, and just generally acting like kids getting ready to surprise their parents.

Everybody who didn't work stood in the doorway and watched, or waited in the sitting room to greet the newcomers and watch their expressions as they saw the quilt spread out across Mary's chair. Most everybody had seen it the day before, but this was different. It was finished. The extra stitches had been cut away, all the little slivers of material brushed aside, the floor vacuumed, the quilt laid out for all to see. People came in and were cautioned to silence on account of the door to the back room being open; then those already there would kind of shuffle aside so the newcomers could see the quilt. There was a little gasp of inward breath, a little step forward with outstretched hand, a moment of silence, and the words everybody'd been waiting to hear. It was a glorious quilt.

Finally the frame was built up again, and the quilt was taken and set into place. By this time the door was jammed so tight with bodies that those in back couldn't see a thing. Everett sat in the chair by the bed, watching it all with eyes that didn't seem to be seeing very much, so quiet and still that after a moment nobody really thought much about him being there.

The side-clamps were tightened and the frame was raised upright, barely fitting in under the ceiling, and another little gasp escaped from the people by the door. The sound woke Mary.

She turned her head slowly toward the noise, and it took a moment for her to realize how many people were there. Then she caught sight of the quilt out of the corner of her eye, and swivelled her head back up-right.

Mary reached a fragile hand out toward

Everett, said in an ancient voice, "Hand me my glasses, son."

"It's done, Momma," Jody said, so ex-

cited she could barely stand it.

At those words the crowd outside pushed the ones in front forward, and more than a dozen people spilled into the room. They moved over toward the bed's head-board so as to be seeing the quilt as Mary did. And the sight was really something, what with the quilt almost big enough to cover the entire back wall. Lou Ann helped Jody slide another pillow under Mary's head so she could see it better. Grins kept popping up all over the room. They'd look from the quilt back to Mary and back to the quilt again, and then show another little grin to their neighbor.

Mary looked at it for a long, long time. She looked at it for so long that people started getting little lumps in their throats, watching her look at the quilt, thinking about how everybody said it would never get done, remembering how they them-

116

selves had labored over this or that, recalling the work, recalling the prayers. Truly, it was a *glorious* quilt.

Finally, Mary turned to look over the friends and family gathered there in her room. She held them there for a moment, returning their smiles and shining eyes with a gaze that seemed to reach deep inside.

With visible effort Mary raised her head up and said with surprising strength, "Now all of you go out there and finish what you've started."

Despite the fact that she was close to being scared out of her wits, Jody went up to the altar alone the morning of Mary's funeral. Lou Ann helped her work out what she was going to say, but there was no way Lou Ann could leave Everett alone just then, especially not at the funeral. Jonas had just plain turned and walked away. When Jody pressed him all he said was, the last time you got me to stand up in front of other people was at our wedding. I don't aim on making a fool of myself twice in one life. Lynn said she'd go up there with her, but she kind of felt in her heart like it was something Jody needed to do alone. Jody was held back from pressing her best friend by the fact that she felt in her heart that Lynn was right.

The church was filled to capacity that morning, was how Reverend Louis put it. The back and side doors were all open to the early summer sun, but any breeze that might have been there to cool off the flock was blocked by the crowd pushing for room to see. Those who got there early enough had a place in the pews and busied themselves fanning up meager puffs of air with hats and programs and prayer book bindings.

The others crowded in a semicircle around the outer walls, content to lean and shift their weight and perch their children up on the windowsills. The only people who weren't crowded were those in the front two rows and the choir. The choir suffered as all choirs do in stuffy summer churches, be-robed and chafing and hoping their sweat didn't drip on the hymnals. Those in the front two rows would have simply given the world to be anywhere but where they were.

Reverend Louis led the congregation through a hymn and a prayer and a short talk about a woman everybody knew, and all the while gave the little white terry-cloth towel he carried in his pocket a real good work out. He thought of something he'd have to share with his wife once it was all over, which was that one could have found more breathing space in an unopened can of sardines than there in that church.

By the time Jody got up, the church was one big fidget. A basket full of week-old puppies would have been calmer. She had a time finding the place in her Bible, what with the perspiration in her eyes and the clammy feeling that left her fingers clumsy. To keep the trembling from showing, Jody slid one finger on the page and grabbed that hand with the other and squeezed. She looked up at the crowd and tried to speak above the fretful babies and the rustling fans and the quiet noise that a crowd makes when it's ready to get up and out but is too polite to say so.

"I know it's gonna sound a little crazy to read a passage of thanks at Momma's funeral," Jody began, and found herself getting all choked up. It was kind of strange, because she hadn't really felt that much grief during the past twenty-four hours. The day before yesterday had been touch and go, but yesterday hadn't been too bad. There'd been one moment in the bathroom last night when she was afraid she was going to drop her youngest, she'd started crying so hard. And that had scared the poor little one so bad she'd been forced to get control over herself. After that she'd been pretty much okay until she was in bed with Jonas, and then the good man had had to rock her to sleep like a little girl.

Jody swallowed real hard and made her eyelids flutter and pinched her hand real good, and fought back the burning behind her eyes. She went on, "But all of us who knew Momma knew she would never want anything else.

"This passage comes from Philippians, chapter four, verses four through seven:

Rejoice in the Lord always. I will say it again: Rejoice! Let your gentleness be

evident to all. The Lord is near. Do not be anxious about anything, but in everything, by prayer and petition, with thanksgiving, present your requests to God. And the peace of God, which transcends all understanding, will guard your hearts and your minds in Christ Jesus.

Jody raised her eyes from the Book and saw that the church had settled. Her own nervousness was lessening, the pressure in her throat totally gone. "There's a lot I could say about the mother of my husband," Jody began. "The lady the world knows as Miss Mary, and who became as close to me as my own mother. But it would just be repeating what you already know. So I'll say what Momma would want me to say, and that is to give thanks to the Lord your God every day. She taught me a lot, more than I could ever say to anybody, but this last lesson of hers is

the one I'll fight hardest to keep. It truly is the way to knowing the peace that surpasses all understanding."

Everybody who came to Mary's little house on the hill after the service stopped by to tell Jody how well she did. It wasn't just nice, someone said, it was like something I'd expect to have Mary say. Wise and sweet and short, somebody else told her, just the thing that Mary would want said. You've given me something to carry with me for a long time, another friend said, one last little gift from Mary.

Lynn came up as she was refilling the punch bowl and said, "Better watch out, honey, there's a delegation in the corner over there ready to put you up for Mary's place."

Now that it was over, the hole was back in Jody's heart. She struggled to make a smile, said, "They've got to be scraping the bottom of the barrel, then."

"I don't know," Lynn said, wearing the same smile she'd had since the service. "It really was a little like Miss Mary, the way you stood up there and talked from the heart."

Jody decided it was time to change the subject. She pointed with her chin toward the quilt stand, said, "Just look at that, will you."

The back wall of Mary's sitting room was hidden by the upright quilt frame. It *dominated* the room, drawing every eye toward it as soon as the outer door was opened.

It was as though the reason for the gathering had to be put aside until the newcomer had gotten up close to the quilt, touched it, admired it, talked to a couple of neighbors about it, gotten lost for a moment in the beauty of the design. Every lag in the conversation was filled with a comment about the quilt.

"It's hard to believe I ever worked on anything that pretty," Lynn agreed.

"I wish there was some way you could see the prayers we sewed into it," Jody said, mostly to herself.

Lynn looked around the room, saw the sadness leave faces as they looked back to the quilt. She turned toward the back wall, saw her neighbors wipe away tears and smile as they reached out and touched the circular flowers.

She patted Jody's arm, said, "Maybe you can."